Tomie dePaola

HEY DIDDLE DIDDLE
DIDDLE & other
Mother Goose Rhymes

G. P. Putnam's Sons

NEW YORK

Wherever possible, the Mother Goose rhymes
in this book are the classic versions collected by peter and Iona opie.

G. P. Putnam's Sons, a division of The Putnam & Grosset Book Group,
200 Madison Avenue, New York, NY 10016.
Sandcastle Books and the Sandcastle logo are trademarks belonging to
The Putnam & Grosset Book Group.
First Sandcastle Books edition, 1988.
Published simultaneously in Canada.
Printed in Hong Kong
L. C. number: 88-11561
5 7 9 10 8 6

INDEX OF FIRST LINES

Simple Simon met a pieman
　　Going to the fair;
Says Simple Simon to the pieman,
　　Let me taste your ware.

Says the pieman to Simple Simon,
　　Show me first your penny;
Says Simple Simon to the pieman,
　　Indeed I have not any.

Simple Simon went a-fishing,
　　For to catch a whale;
All the water he had got
　　Was in his mother's pail.

He went to catch a dickey bird,
    And thought he could not fail,
Because he'd got a little salt,
    To put upon its tail.

Once Simon made a great snowball,
    And brought it in to roast;
He laid it down before the fire,
    And soon the ball was lost.

He went for water in a sieve,
    But soon it all ran through;
And now poor Simple Simon
    Bids you all adieu.

Baa, baa, black sheep,
Have you any wool?
Yes, sir, yes, sir,
Three bags full;
One for the master,
And one for the dame,
And one for the little boy
Who lives down the lane.

The cock's on the roof top
  Blowing his horn,
The bull's in the barn
  A-threshing the corn,
The maids in the meadow
  Are making the hay,
The ducks in the river
  Are swimming away.

Come, butter, come,
Come, butter, come;
Peter stands at the gate
Waiting for a butter cake.
Come, butter, come.

Knock on the door,
    Peek in.
Lift up the latch,
    And walk in.

Pat-a-cake, pat-a-cake, baker's man,
Bake me a cake as fast as you can;
Pat it and prick it, and mark it with T,
Put it in the oven for Tommy and me.

Bye, baby bunting,
Daddy's gone a-hunting,
Gone to get a rabbit skin
To wrap the baby bunting in.

Hickory, dickory, dock,
The mouse ran up the clock.
The clock struck one,
The mouse ran down,
Hickory, dickory, dock.

There was a rat, for want of stairs,
Went down a rope to say his prayers.

There were once two cats of Kilkenny.
Each thought there was one cat too many;
So they fought and they fit,
And they scratched and they bit,
Till, excepting their nails,
And the tips of their tails,
Instead of two cats, there weren't any.

Old Mother Hubbard
Went to the cupboard,
To fetch her poor dog a bone;
But when she got there
The cupboard was bare
And so the poor dog had none.

She went to the baker's
To buy him some bread;
But when she came back
The poor dog was dead.

She went to the undertaker's
To buy him a coffin;
But when she came back
The poor dog was laughing.

She took a clean dish
To get him some tripe;
But when she came back
He was smoking a pipe.

She went to the fishmonger's
To buy him some fish;
But when she came back
He was licking the dish.

She went to the tavern
For white wine and red;
But when she came back
The dog stood on his head.

She went to the fruiterer's
To buy him some fruit;
But when she came back
He was playing the flute.

She went to the tailor's
    To buy him a coat;
But when she came back
    He was riding a goat.

She went to the hatter's
    To buy him a hat;
But when she came back
    He was feeding the cat.

She went to the barber's
    To buy him a wig;
But when she came back
    He was dancing a jig.

She went to the cobbler's
    To buy him some shoes;
But when she came back
    He was reading the news.

She went to the seamstress
    To buy him some linen;
But when she came back
    The dog was a-spinning.

She went to the hosier's
    To buy him some hose;
But when she came back
    He was dressed in his clothes.

The dame made a curtsey,
    The dog made a bow;
The dame said, Your Servant,
    The dog said, Bow-bow.

Dickery, dickery, dare,
The pig flew up in the air;
The man in brown
Soon brought him down,
Dickery, dickery, dare.

Rub-a-dub-dub,
Three men in a tub,
And how do you think they got there?
The butcher, the baker,
The candlestick-maker,
They all jumped out of a rotten
potato,
'Twas enough to make a man stare.

Polly put the kettle on,
Polly put the kettle on,
Polly put the kettle on,
    We'll all have tea.

Sukey take it off again,
Sukey take it off again,
Sukey take it off again,
    They've all gone away.

Roses are red,
    Violets are blue,
Sugar is sweet
    And so are you.

This little pig went to market,
This little pig stayed at home,
This little pig had roast beef,
This little pig had none,
And this little pig cried, Wee-wee-
    wee-wee-wee,
I can't find my way home.

Jack and Jill
Went up the hill,
To fetch a pail of water;
Jack fell down,
And broke his crown,
And Jill came tumbling after.

Then up Jack got,
And home did trot,
As fast as he could caper;
To old Dame Dob,
Who patched his nob
With vinegar and brown paper.

When Jill came in,
How she did grin
To see Jack's paper plaster;
Her mother, vexed,
Did whip her next,
For laughing at Jack's disaster.

Now Jack did laugh
And Jill did cry,
But her tears did soon abate;
Then Jill did say,
That they should play
At see-saw across the gate.

1, 2,
Buckle my shoe;

3, 4,
Knock at the door;

5, 6,
Pick up sticks;

7, 8,
Lay them straight;

9, 10,
A big fat hen;

11, 12,
Dig and delve;

13, 14,
Maids a-courting;

15, 16,
Maids in the kitchen;

17, 18,
Maids in waiting;

19, 20,
My plate's empty.

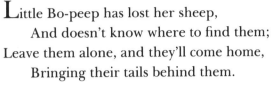
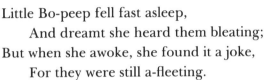

Little Bo-peep has lost her sheep,
    And doesn't know where to find them;
Leave them alone, and they'll come home,
    Bringing their tails behind them.

Little Bo-peep fell fast asleep,
    And dreamt she heard them bleating;
But when she awoke, she found it a joke,
    For they were still a-fleeting.

Then up she took her little crook,
    Determined for to find them;
She found them indeed, but it made her heart bleed
    For they'd left their tails behind them.

It happened one day, as Bo-peep did stray
    Into a meadow hard by,
There she espied their tails side by side,
    All hung on a tree to dry.

She heaved a sigh, and wiped her eye,
    And over the hillocks went rambling,
And tried what she could, as a shepherdess should,
    To tack again each to its lambkin.

The north wind doth blow,
And we shall have snow,
And what will poor Robin do then,
    Poor thing?
He'll sit in a barn,
And keep himself warm,
And hide his head under his wing,
    Poor thing.

Rain before seven,
Fine before eleven.

Rain, rain, go away,
Come again another day,
Little Johnny wants to play.
Rain, rain, go to Spain,
Never show your face again.

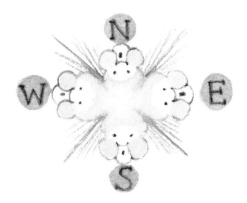

When the wind is in the east,
'Tis neither good for man nor beast;
When the wind is in the north,
The skilful fisher goes not forth;
When the wind is in the south,
It blows the bait in the fishes' mouth;
When the wind is in the west,
Then 'tis at the very best.

March winds and April showers
Bring forth May flowers.

Red sky at night,
Shepherd's delight;
Red sky in the morning,
Shepherd's warning.

Goosey, goosey gander,
    Whither shall I wander?
Upstairs and downstairs
    And in my lady's chamber.
There I met an old man
    Who would not say his prayers,
I took him by the left leg
    And threw him down the stairs.

Hickety, pickety, my black hen,
She lays eggs for gentlemen;
Gentlemen come every day
To see what my black hen doth lay.

Cock a doodle doo!
My dame has lost her shoe,
My master's lost his fiddling stick
And knows not what to do.

Cock a doodle doo!
What is my dame to do?
Till master finds his fiddling stick
She'll dance without her shoe.

Cock a doodle doo!
My dame has found her shoe,
And master's found his fiddling stick,
Sing doodle doodle doo.

Cock a doodle doo!
My dame will dance with you,
While master fiddles his fiddling stick
For dame and doodle doo.

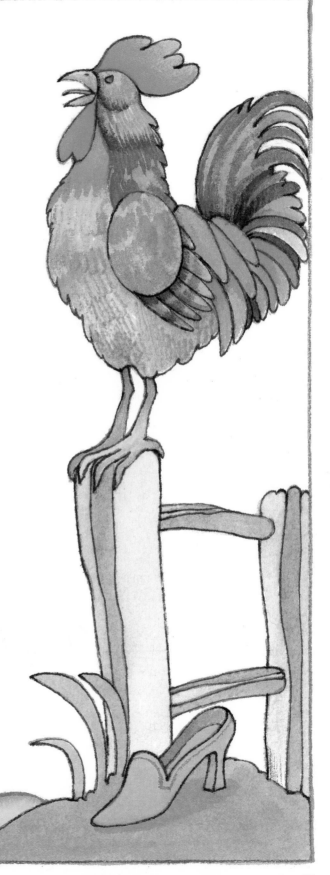

Georgie Porgie, pudding and pie,
Kissed the girls and made them cry;
When the boys came out to play,
Georgie Porgie ran away.

Little Miss Muffet
Sat on a tuffet,
Eating her curds and whey;
There came a big spider,
Who sat down beside her
And frightened Miss Muffet away.

Peter, Peter, pumpkin eater,
Had a wife and couldn't keep her;
He put her in a pumpkin shell
And there he kept her very well.

Tom, Tom, the piper's son,
Stole a pig and away he run;
The pig was eat,
And Tom was beat,
And Tom went howling down the street.

Humpty Dumpty sat on a wall,
Humpty Dumpty had a great fall;
All the King's horses and all the King's men
Couldn't put Humpty together again.

Mary, Mary, quite contrary,
How does your garden grow?
With silver bells and cockle shells,
And pretty maids all in a row.

There was an old woman who lived in a shoe,
She had so many children she didn't know what to do;
She gave them some broth without any bread;
She whipped them all soundly and put them to bed.

See-saw, Margery Daw,
Jacky shall have a new master;
Jacky shall have but a penny a day,
Because he can't work any faster.

Little girl, little girl,
 Where have you been?
I've been to see grandmother
 Over the green.
What did she give you?
 Milk in a can.
What did you say for it?
 Thank you, Grandam.

What are little boys made of, made of?
What are little boys made of?
 Frogs and snails
 And puppy-dogs' tails,
That's what little boys are made of.

What are little girls made of, made of?
What are little girls made of?
 Sugar and spice
 And all things nice,
That's what little girls are made of.

Old King Cole
Was a merry old soul,
And a merry old soul was he;
He called for his pipe,
And he called for his bowl,
And he called for his fiddlers three.

Every fiddler he had a fiddle,
And a very fine fiddle had he;
Oh, there's none so rare
As can compare
With King Cole and his fiddlers three.

Hey diddle, diddle,
The cat and the fiddle,
The cow jumped over the moon;
The little dog laughed
To see such sport,
And the dish ran away with the spoon.

Barber, barber, shave a pig,
How many hairs will make a wig?
Four and twenty, that's enough.
Give the barber a pinch of snuff.

Bow, wow, wow,
Whose dog art thou?
Little Tom Tinker's dog,
Bow, wow, wow.

The lion and the unicorn
    Were fighting for the crown;
The lion beat the unicorn
    All around the town.

Some gave them white bread,
    And some gave them brown;
Some gave them plum cake
    And drummed them out of town.

Hush-a-bye, baby, on the tree top,
When the wind blows the cradle will rock;
When the bough breaks the cradle will fall,
Down will come baby, cradle, and all.

When little Fred went to bed,
He always said his prayers;
He kissed mamma, and then papa,
And straightway went upstairs.

The Man in the Moon looked out of the moon,
Looked out of the moon and said,
"'Tis time for all children on the earth
To think about getting to bed!"

Wee Willie Winkie runs through the town,
Upstairs and downstairs in his night-gown,
Rapping at the window, crying through the lock,
Are the children all in bed, for now it's eight o'clock?

Now I lay me down to sleep,
I pray the Lord my soul to keep;
And if I die before I wake,
I pray the Lord my soul to take.